EVERY YEAR, ON THE FEAST OF THE THREE KINGS, January the sixth, Old Befana visits all the children of Italy and leaves them candies, cookies, and gifts. It is said that she is searching for the Christ Child.

There are many stories about Old Befana and how she began her search.

This is one of them.

The LEGEND of OLD BEFANA

An Italian Christmas story
retold and illustrated by

TOMIE dePAOLA

SIMON & SCHUSTER BOOKS FOR YOUNG READERS

NEW YORK   LONDON   TORONTO   SYDNEY   NEW DELHI

For Coleen Salley

 SIMON & SCHUSTER BOOKS FOR YOUNG READERS
An imprint of Simon & Schuster Children's Publishing Division
1230 Avenue of the Americas, New York, New York 10020
Copyright © 1980 by Tomie dePaola
All rights reserved, including the right of reproduction in whole or in part in any form.
SIMON & SCHUSTER BOOKS FOR YOUNG READERS is a trademark of Simon & Schuster, Inc.
For information about special discounts for bulk purchases,
please contact Simon & Schuster Special Sales at 1-866-506-1949 or business@simonandschuster.com.
The Simon & Schuster Speakers Bureau can bring authors to your live event.
For more information or to book an event, contact the Simon & Schuster Speakers Bureau
at 1-866-248-3049 or visit our website at www.simonspeakers.com.
Also available in a Simon & Schuster Books for Young Readers hardcover edition
Book design by Laurent Linn
The text for this book was set in ITC Cerigo Std.
The illustrations for this book were rendered in colored inks and watercolor
on Cotman 140 lb. handmade watercolor paper.
Manufactured in China
0719 SCP
This Simon & Schuster Books for Young Readers paperback edition September 2019
2 4 6 8 10 9 7 5 3 1
The Library of Congress has cataloged the hardcover edition as follows:
Names: DePaola, Tomie, 1934– author illustrator.
Title: The legend of Old Befana : an Italian Christmas story / retold and illustrated by Tomie dePaola.
Description: First Simon & Schuster Books for Young Readers edition. | New York : Simon & Schuster Books for Young Readers,
[2017] | Summary: Because Befana's household chores kept her from finding the Baby King, she searches to this day,
leaving gifts for children on the Feast of the Three Kings.
Identifiers: LCCN 2016039502 | ISBN 9781481477635 (hardcover) | ISBN 9781534430112 (pbk) | ISBN 9781481477642 (ebook)
Subjects: LCSH: Befana (Legendary character)—Juvenile literature. | CYAC: Befana (Legendary character) |
Folklore—Italy. | Christmas—Folklore.
Classification: LCC PZ8.1.D43 Le 2017 | DDC 398.2 [E] —dc23 LC record available at https://lccn.loc.gov/2016039502

In a small house, on the outskirts of a small village in Italy, lived Old Befana.

She lived all alone, and she wasn't very friendly.

If any people dared to knock at her door, she never asked them in.

"I have no time for visiting," Old Befana would say.

The children didn't like her either.

"Cranky old lady," they said. "And the way she is always *sweeping*!"

That was true.
Every day, every morning and afternoon,
Old Befana would sweep with her broom.

She swept her little house.
She swept her front step.
And she even swept her walk, all the way
down to the road.

Sometimes a delicious smell of things baking would drift from Old Befana's house.

"Whom does she bake for?" her neighbors would ask.

And some nights, they thought they heard her singing lullabies.

"Crazy Old Befana," everybody called her.

One evening, after Old Befana had eaten her dinner and swept her kitchen clean, she began to get ready for bed. She locked the door and shuttered the windows.

Then she climbed into her bed, blew out the lamp, and fell asleep.

In the middle of the night, Old Befana woke up.
The room was bright.

"How can that be?" she asked. "My lamp is out,
my windows are shuttered, but still my house is filled
with light."

She got out of bed and crossed the cold floor.

When she opened the shutter, a sudden burst of
light poured into the room.

In the eastern sky she saw a brilliant star, which
seemed to grow before her eyes.

"Hurumph!" said Old Befana, closing the shutter as
tightly as she could. "How am I ever to get my sleep
when the dark has turned to day?"

All night she tossed and turned.

She didn't sleep a wink.

At dawn, Old Befana got up and dressed.

She ate her breakfast, then took her broom, as she always did, every day, every morning and afternoon.

She swept her little house.

She swept her front step.

She even swept the walk all the way down to the road.

When she neared the road, Old Befana stopped and listened.

She heard bells tinkling.
"It's probably just the wind," she said.
Sweep, sweep, sweep.
Again! She heard the bells.
"It's probably just the birds singing."
Sweep, sweep, sweep.
Once more she heard the sound.
"My old ears play tricks," she said.
Sweep, sweep . . .

Suddenly, over the hill, came the most glorious
procession Old Befana had ever seen.
Camels, horses, elephants, and people.

A splendid sight!
Halfway back rode three royal-looking men, dressed in jeweled robes, wearing crowns upon their heads.

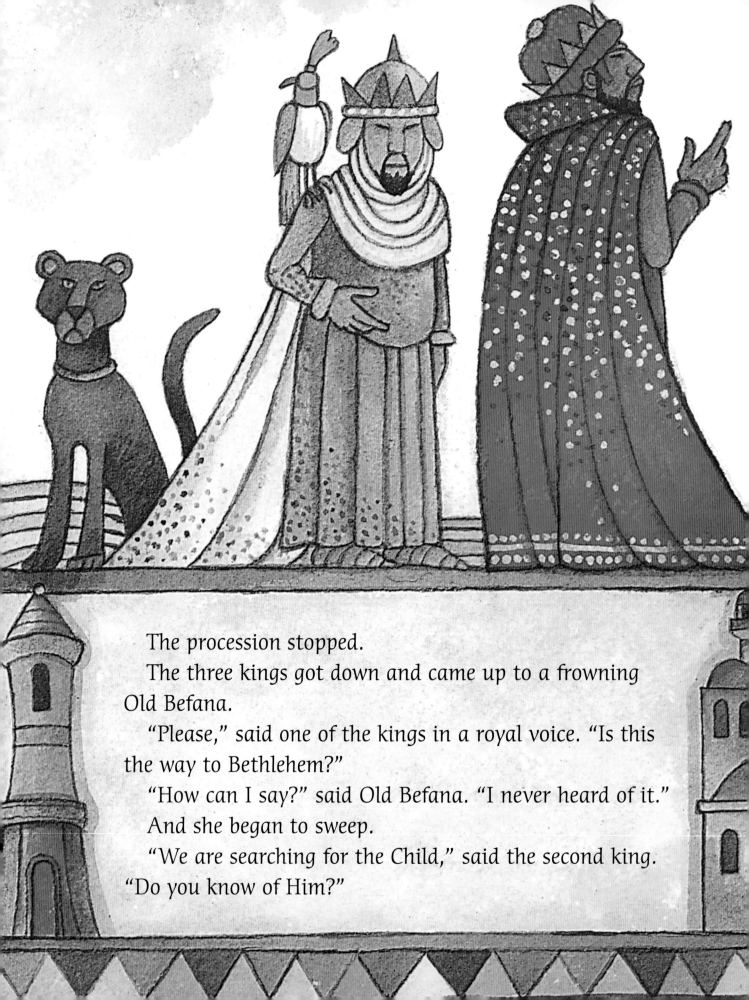

The procession stopped.

The three kings got down and came up to a frowning Old Befana.

"Please," said one of the kings in a royal voice. "Is this the way to Bethlehem?"

"How can I say?" said Old Befana. "I never heard of it." And she began to sweep.

"We are searching for the Child," said the second king. "Do you know of Him?"

"There are many children," said Old Befana, sweeping still.
"But this one is a King," said the third.
"I know nothing of royal matters," she said.
"Our books have told us," said the kings, "that when a bright new star appears, the Child King will be born in Bethlehem."
"The star I have seen," said Old Befana. "It kept me awake all night. Now—if you will excuse me, I have work to do."

The procession started up again.

"Old woman," called a boy who was leading a camel by. "You should come with us. This Child, this Baby King, has come to change the world. He comes for us. He comes for the poor. We are bringing Him gifts."

Old Befana paused.

She watched the procession wind down the road.
"A Child King," she muttered. "Bethlehem . . ."
Sweep, sweep, sweep.
"Coming to change the world. Coming for the poor.
Well, heaven knows, Old Befana is poor."
Sweep, sweep . . .
". . . gifts. Only a Child . . ."

Old Befana went back into her house.
"Perhaps I should go see Him . . . but what do I have
to take Him?"
She put down her broom.
She got out some butter, and sugar and flour.
She blew on the fire and added some wood.
And she began to sing.

She baked all day.
She didn't even sweep.
It was almost dark when she finished.
Then she filled a basket with all the cakes, cookies, and candies she had made.
"I'll take a few coals in a little pot to keep the cookies warm," she said.

She put on a shawl and opened the door.

"And I'll take along my broom to sweep the room clean, for the Baby King's mother will be tired."

Old Befana stopped.

She hadn't swept all day.

"It won't take me long," she said.
She put down the basket and began to sweep.
She swept her little house.
She swept her front step.
And she even swept her walk all the way down
to the road.

Then she locked her door and gathered up her basket.
She pulled her shawl around her and took up her broom.
Old Befana was on her way at last.
She ran at first, ran and ran, as fast as her legs would
carry her.
The sun had set.
But still she ran.
Now the star shone brightly.

Her breath came short, her old legs ached, but still she ran, a little bit slower.

At last she sat beside the road.

Old Befana could run no more.

"I should have left earlier. I'll never catch up," she cried. "And where is Bethlehem?"

She closed her eyes and gave a long sigh.

"I'll never find the Baby King."

Suddenly the sky was filled with light, and heavenly angels sang.

"Glory to all men. The new King is born. Tonight is the night of miracles!"

Old Befana rose to her feet.

"Tell me! Tell me where He is," she cried, picking up her basket and broom. "I bring gifts to the Child!"

She began to walk, then run again.

"This is the night of miracles," the angels sang once more.

"Wait," she shouted. "You must help me. Show me the way to Bethlehem!"

Old Befana began to feel lighter.

She ran faster and faster, so fast it took her breath away.

SHE WAS RUNNING IN THE SKY!

. . . It was a night of miracles.

Old Befana never caught up, alas.
She never found the Child in Bethlehem.
But she is searching still, to this day.
Every year on the Feast of the Three Kings,
January the sixth, Old Befana runs across the sky.

She visits all children while they sleep and leaves them gifts from her basket.

Then she takes her broom and sweeps the room all clean.

"For, after all," says Old Befana, "I never know which child might be the Baby King of Bethlehem."

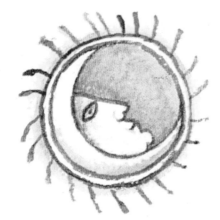